I See a Bat

PAUL MEISEL

I Like to Read®

HOLIDAY HOUSE • NEW YORK

In memory of my dad

I LIKE TO READ is a registered trademark of Holiday House Publishing, Inc.

Text and illustrations copyright © 2023 by Paul Meisel
All Rights Reserved
HOLIDAY HOUSE is registered in the U.S. Patent and Trademark Office.
Printed and bound in December 2022 at C&C Offset, Shenzhen, China.
The artwork was created with watercolor, acrylic, and pencil
on Saunders Waterford paper with digital enhancements.
www.holidayhouse.com
First Edition
1 3 5 7 9 10 8 6 4 2

This book has been officially leveled by using the F&P Text Level Gradient™ Leveling System.

Library of Congress Cataloging-in-Publication Data

Names: Meisel, Paul, author.
Title: I see a bat / Paul Meisel.
Description: First edition. | New York : Holiday House, 2023. | Series: I
like to read | Audience: Ages 4–8. | Audience: Grades K–1. | Summary: A
dog stays up all night, watching the moon and some bats, and looks
forward to the morning when his boy will wake up and feed him breakfast.
Identifiers: LCCN 2022015000 | ISBN 9780823452651 (hardcover)
Subjects: CYAC: Dogs—Fiction. | LCGFT: Picture books.
Classification: LCC PZ7.M5158752 Iak 2023 | DDC [E]—dc23
LC record available at https://lccn.loc.gov/2022015000

ISBN: 978-0-8234-5265-1 (hardcover)

I see a bat.

I see stars.

I see the moon.

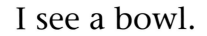

I see a bowl.

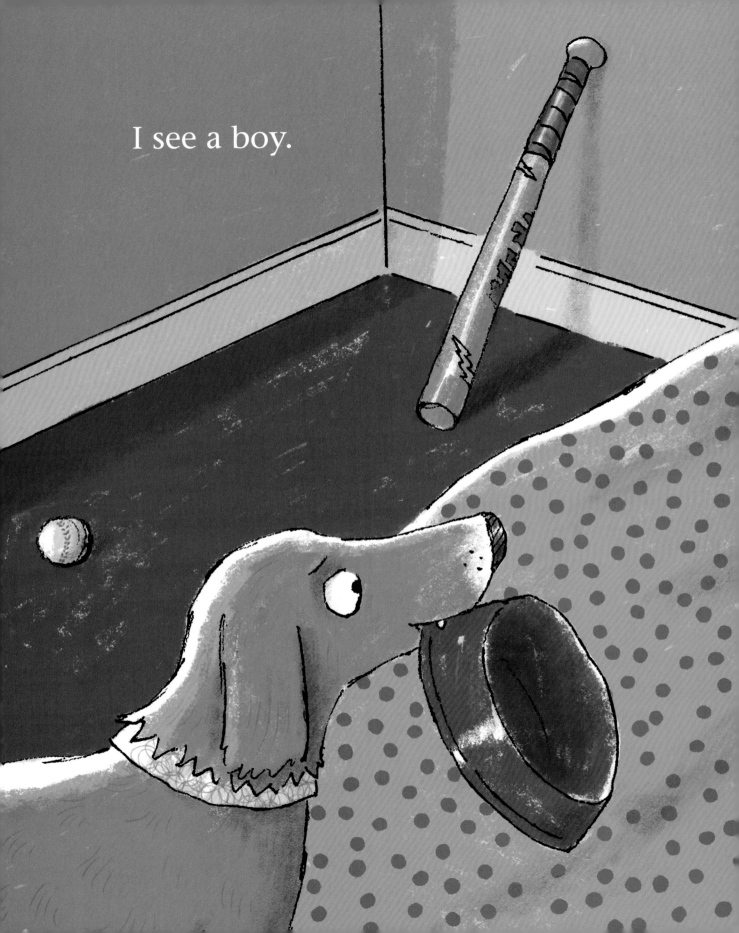

I see a boy.

ZZZZZZZ

I see bats.

I see the sun.

I see a boy.

ALSO BY PAUL MEISEL

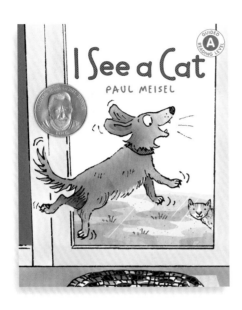

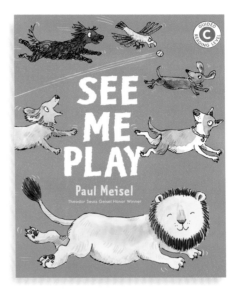

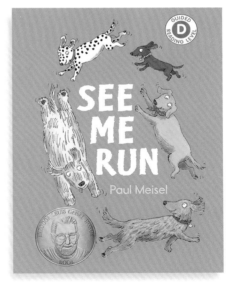

POWERFUL MEDICINE

WOUNDED BRAINS

TRUE SURVIVAL STORIES

SANDRA MARKLE

LERNER PUBLICATIONS COMPANY · MINNEAPOLIS

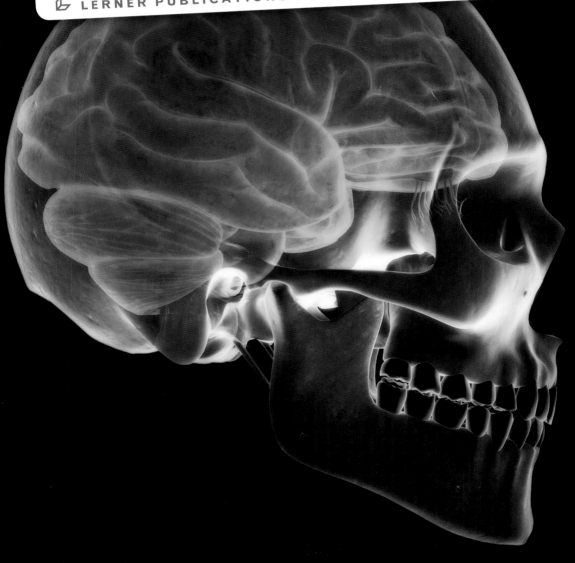

NOTE FROM THE AUTHOR

The books in the Powerful Medicine series are the result of exciting detective work that let me talk to amazing, caring physicians, surgeons, and researchers. I also got to know patients who faced challenging, life-changing experiences with great determination. I consider all the people you'll meet in the Powerful Medicine series heroes—their stories are remarkable. Those you'll meet in *Wounded Brains* are also courageous. They've had to learn to live with changed abilities to think and function, even changed personalities, and memories.

FOR CURIOUS KIDS EVERYWHERE—THEY'RE THE FUTURE!

Acknowledgments: The author would like to thank the following people for taking the time to share their expertise: Dr. Charles Cox, Department of Biomedical Engineering, University of Texas Medical School, Houston; Dr. Thomas Glenn, Department of Neurosurgery, David Geffen School of Medicine at University of California-Los Angeles; Matthew Morris, rehabilitation therapist at Albert Einstein Medical Center, New York City; Dr. Douglas Smith, director of the Center for Brain Injury and Repair, professor of neurosurgery at the University of Pennsylvania in Philadelphia; Dr. Bruce Spiess, principal investigator and VCURES director, Virginia Commonwealth University in Richmond, Virginia; Dr. Donald Stein, Asa G. Candler professor of Emergency Medicine, Neurology and Psychobiology, at the Emory University School of Medicine in Atlanta, Georgia; Dr. Jonathan Pascoe, Ilam Medical Centre, Christchurch, New Zealand. A special thank-you to Skip Jeffery for his loving support during the creative process.

Lerner Publications Company
A division of Lerner Publishing Group, Inc.
241 First Avenue North
Minneapolis, MN 55401 U.S.A.

Website address: www.lernerbooks.com

Library of Congress Cataloging-in-Publication Data

Markle, Sandra.
　　Wounded brains / by Sandra Markle.
　　　　p.　cm. — (Powerful medicine)
　　Includes bibliographical references and index.
　　ISBN 978–0–8225–8704–0 (lib. bdg. : alk. paper)
　　1. Brain damage—Juvenile literature. 2. Brain—Physiology—Juvenile literature. I. Title.
RC387.5.M369 2011
617.4′81044—dc22　　　　　　　　　　　　　　　2009034440

Manufactured in the United States of America
1 – DP – 7/15/10

CONTENTS

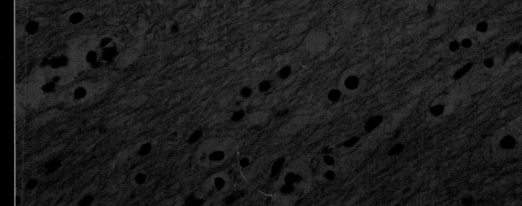

We go through life without thinking about how our bodies work to keep us healthy and active. Then something happens and we realize the importance of the part that is damaged or not functioning properly. **One of those key parts is our brain.** In this book, you will find dramatic, real-life stories of people who have suffered a severe brain injury. The stories tell of the efforts of doctors and medical researchers to help them live full, productive lives afterward. The tales also show how science and technology are helping to make these efforts possible.

CRASH!

CANDACE GANTT PEDALED FASTER, pulling ahead of her friend and training partner, Mary Wood. It was spring 2005, and Candace was in training for the Wilkes-Barre Triathlon held annually near her home in Berwyn, Pennsylvania. Candace was focused on keeping up her speed while climbing a hill. A cement truck that had been following her suddenly roared up alongside attempting to pass her. The truck's rear bumper struck her bicycle and sent her flying. She tumbled through the air and crashed onto the highway, hitting her head against the pavement. Even though she had a helmet on, the blow had a severe effect. **It caused her brain to slam into the inside of her skull.**

Mary quickly phoned for help. Candace was unconscious when emergency crews arrived. She was airlifted by helicopter to the University of Pennsylvania Trauma Center in Philadelphia. Candace was still unconscious when she arrived at the hospital. She was in a coma. That meant she couldn't be awakened and didn't respond in any way. She had suffered a traumatic brain injury (TBI).

TRAUMATIC BRAIN INJURY IS DAMAGE TO THE BRAIN THAT OCCURS WHEN A PERSON'S HEAD IS HIT, SHAKEN HARD, OR PUNCTURED. The injury affects how the brain functions. It may also change how the person acts, moves, and thinks.

There are two types of head injuries—open and closed. Either can cause a TBI. An open head injury happens when something breaks through the skull. For example, in 1998 Travis Bogumill suffered an open head injury while remodeling a house. He walked under a ladder just as another worker climbed down with a nail gun. The nail gun bumped Travis's head and fired a nail into his skull, damaging his brain. Travis recovered. But years later, he still has trouble doing some things, including solving math problems. Before the accident, Travis was a math whiz.

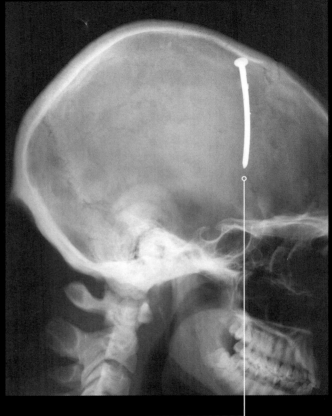

This X-ray shows a 3.25-inch (8.3 centimeter) nail that had to be surgically removed from Travis's skull.

A closed head injury happens when something strikes the head, the head hits something, or the head rotates too rapidly. The skull itself is hard bone. Inside the skull, the brain is similar to firmly set gelatin. In 2005 Chelsea Davis hit her head on a springboard while diving at the World Aquatics Championships. The impact jolted her brain inside her skull like shaken Jell-O. The brain striking against the bony skull caused bruising, and the brain tissue was damaged. It took almost three years for Chelsea to completely recover from this brain injury. After that she was again able to compete as a diver.

WORLDWIDE, TBI IS ONE OF THE LEADING CAUSES OF DEATHS AMONG PEOPLE UNDER THE AGE OF FORTY-FIVE.

The blood on Chelsea's face is from scrapes and cuts she suffered when she hit the springboard while diving.

Candace suffered a closed TBI. Doctors feared that broken blood vessels in Candace's brain would cause severe problems. Whenever soft tissue, such as the brain, is damaged, blood leaks out of the damaged tissue's blood vessels. It pours into the surrounding areas, making them swell. But there's no room inside the skull for this swollen tissue. It gets squeezed between other parts of the brain and the bony skull. This pressure can further damage the tissue being squeezed. The type of damage depends on what area of the brain is put under pressure.

The white area in this brain scan shows a hematoma, a mass of pooled blood in the brain.

WHEN THE BRAIN SWELLS

DOCTORS WORRIED CANDACE'S BRAIN STEM COULD BE DAMAGED BY HER BRAIN TISSUE SWELLING. The brain stem is at the base of the skull. It is a small part of the brain, but it is necessary to life. All signals coming to or leaving the brain pass through it. **The brain stem controls all the body's automatic functions.** These include breathing, the rate the heart beats, swallowing, digestion, and consciousness.

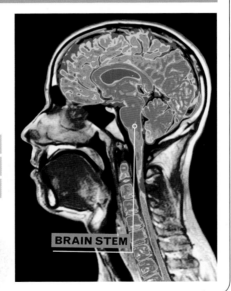

BRAIN STEM

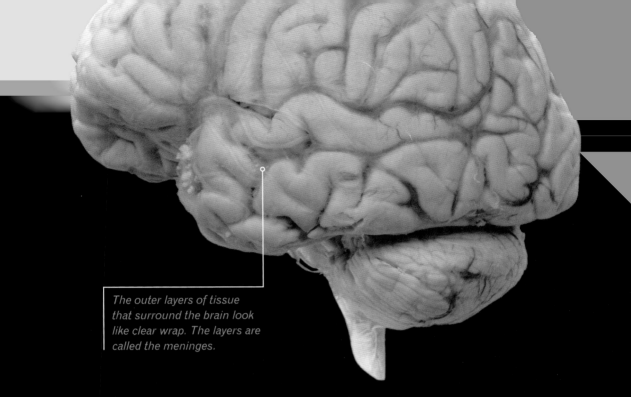

The outer layers of tissue that surround the brain look like clear wrap. The layers are called the meninges.

Three layers of tissue cover the brain. The three layers together are called the meninges. The inner layer, called the pia mater, surrounds the brain like a sac. The space between the pia mater and the brain is filled with a fluid called cerebrospinal fluid. This fluid cushions the brain from shocks and bumps. When brain tissue is damaged, a network of blood vessels inside the brain produces even more cerebrospinal fluid. This extra fluid also causes swelling, which further increases pressure on delicate brain tissue. This can lead to seizures (convulsions or loss of consciousness), dizziness, loss of memory, irregular breathing, loss of vision, and other problems. The problems depend on what part of the brain is put under pressure.

To monitor the pressure on Candace's brain, her medical team used an intracranial pressure monitor. They drilled a small hole into her skull, inserted the small cable-shaped monitor, and screwed in a bolt to keep the monitor in place. The monitor was inserted just deep enough to touch the outer layer of the meninges.

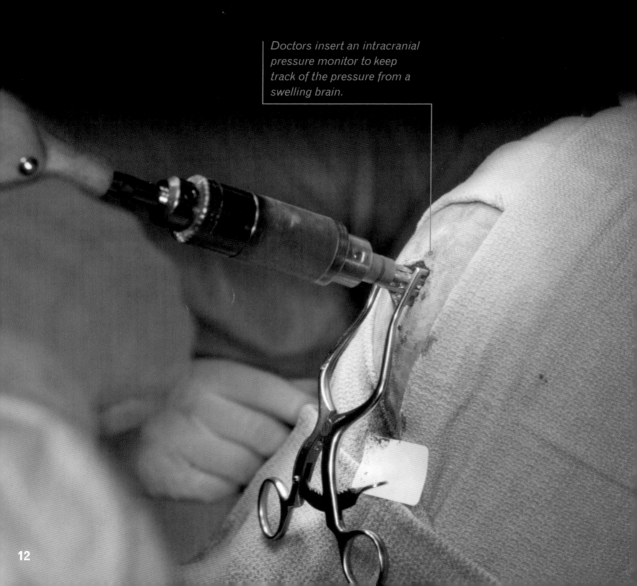

Doctors insert an intracranial pressure monitor to keep track of the pressure from a swelling brain.

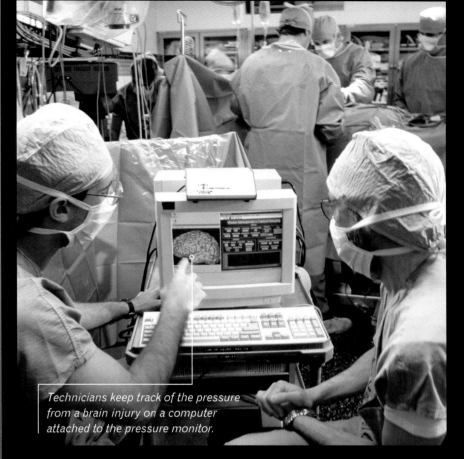

Technicians keep track of the pressure from a brain injury on a computer attached to the pressure monitor.

The monitor measured how much force was pressing against this layer. The greater the force, the greater the pressure on the brain. By late that evening, the pressure on Candace's brain had become so great she was rushed into surgery to relieve it.

The medical team removed a section of Candace's skull the size of a hand to release the pressure on her brain. This piece of skull was placed in cold storage to preserve it. Once her brain had healed, the piece of skull was replaced.

A TRAUMATIC BRAIN INJURY AFFECTS NEURONS, THE NERVE CELLS THAT MAKE UP BRAIN TISSUE. Neurons are surrounded, supported, and held in place by clusters of cells called glial cells. Electrical signals from the brain enter neurons directly or through branchlike dendrites. The signals pass through the nerve cell body and are directed to other neurons through long, thin fibers called axons.

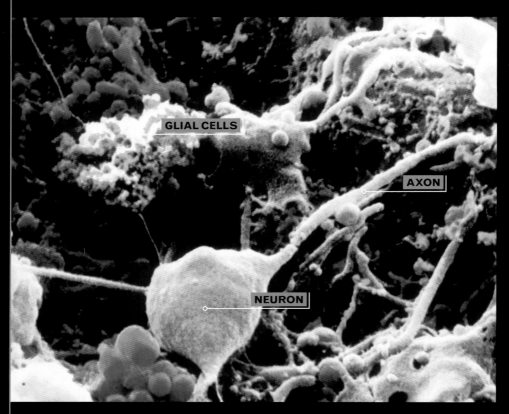

GLIAL CELLS

AXON

NEURON

Axons are wrapped in a protective coat of shiny, white fat, called myelin. Myelin works like the insulation on electrical wires to keep signals traveling smoothly along neuron pathways.

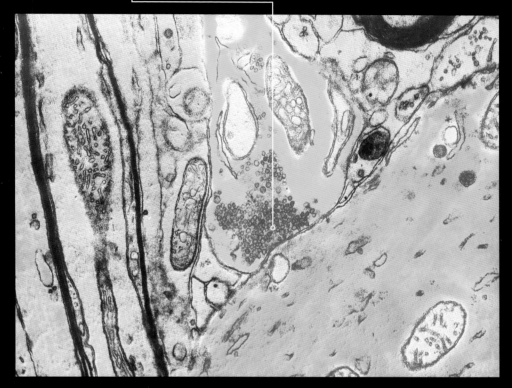

This is a highly magnified view of a neuron's axon almost touching another neuron's dendrite. The tiny red dots are the bits of the chemical that bridge the microscopic gap.

Each time an electrical signal zips along a neuron's axon, it triggers a burst of chemicals. For a fraction of a second, these chemicals bridge the gap to the neighboring neuron. That chemical bridge is called a synapse. A synapse allows the electrical signal from one neuron to travel to the neighboring neuron. Pathways of neurons allow the brain to communicate with the rest of the body.

Dr. Doug Smith says, "During a traumatic event, the brain is rapidly pushed and pulled. This stretches axons and breaks them. Then they swell up like balloons and disconnect. Wherever this damage happens in the brain, neuron signal pathways are disrupted forever."

TRAUMATIC BRAIN INJURY AFFECTS EVERYTHING

AN INJURY TO THE BRAIN IS LIKELY TO AFFECT THE ENTIRE BODY. The brain is the control center for the body's nervous system. Nerves (bundles of fibers made up of neurons) form pathways between the brain and the rest of the body. Some nerves carry signals to the brain from different parts of the body. These include signals from sensory receptors, like the ones in the eyes and ears. The brain helps the eyes and ears make sense of the signals. Other nerves carry signals from the brain to the body's parts.

The spinal cord is the body's main nerve trunk line. **It connects the brain with nerves coming and going to every body part.** The spinal cord also handles some emergency actions. If you touch something hot, for example, the signals from your spinal cord make you jerk away even before the pain signal reaches your brain.

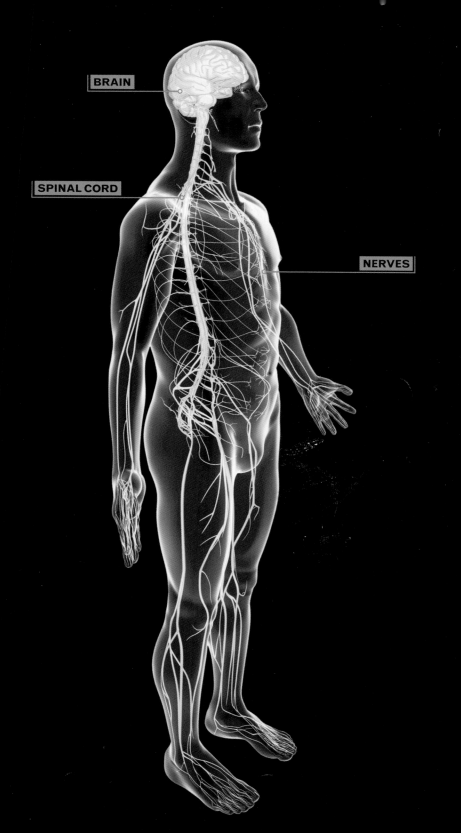

BRAIN

SPINAL CORD

NERVES

Two weeks following the surgery to release the pressure on her brain, Candace woke up. She said, "At first, I could only remember bits of what was going on around me. And from day to day, I was only able to remember moments—like snapshots—of different events."

Traumatic brain injuries may be mild, moderate, or severe. Candace had suffered a severe TBI. The level of injury is judged by studying different factors, such as how long the person was in a coma. Neurologists, doctors who specialize in the nervous system, check how long it takes for the person to start remembering things. They also check if the patient can identify objects and people and if they seem confused. Every person who suffers a traumatic brain injury is affected differently. The problems they experience depend on what parts of the brain are damaged and the extent of the damage to that area.

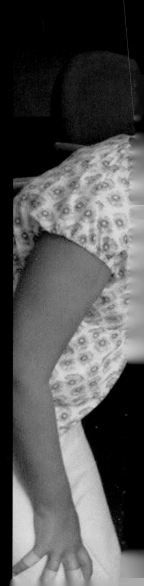

With part of her skull removed, Candace had to wear a helmet to protect her brain whenever she got out of bed. Once that part of her skull was replaced nearly a year later, she no longer had to wear the helmet.

Different parts of the brain analyze and control different body functions. Below are examples of major parts of the brain and the problems people may experience when they are damaged.

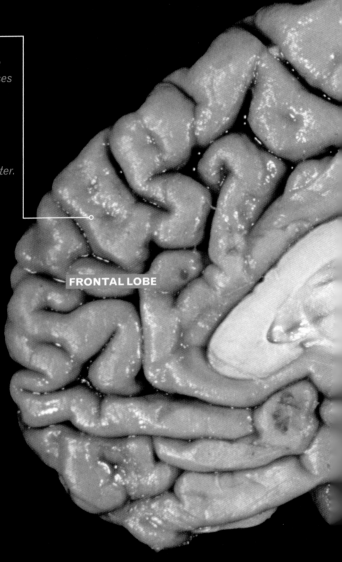

CEREBRUM

The cerebrum is the large part of the brain that controls body movement and responses to senses. It also controls thinking, reasoning, memory, and emotions. The cerebrum has one right and one left hemisphere (side). Each hemisphere is divided into four lobes. The surface of the cerebrum, or cortex, is called the gray matter. The interior of the cerebrum is called the white matter. Damage to each lobe of the cerebrum causes different problems.

LOBES OF THE CEREBRAL HEMISPHERES

FRONTAL LOBE

Damage to the frontal lobe leads to an inability to plan, organize, and reason. A person's personality may also change.

TEMPORAL LOBE

Damage to the temporal lobe causes the loss of short-term memory (the things you do every day like brush your teeth and get dressed). Damage to this lobe makes it hard to recognize faces and objects. It also makes problem-solving difficult.

PARIETAL LOBE

Damage to the parietal lobe makes it difficult to identify objects, to understand the meanings of words, or to tell left from right and up from down.

OCCIPITAL LOBE

Damage to the occipital lobe causes problems in seeing and may cause hallucinations (seeing things that aren't really there).

FRONTAL LOBE

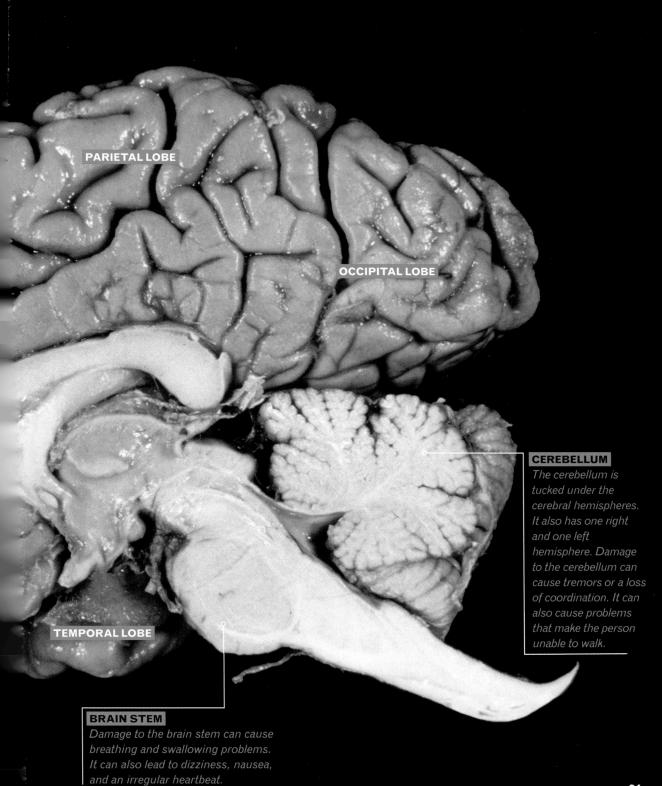

PARIETAL LOBE

OCCIPITAL LOBE

CEREBELLUM
The cerebellum is tucked under the cerebral hemispheres. It also has one right and one left hemisphere. Damage to the cerebellum can cause tremors or a loss of coordination. It can also cause problems that make the person unable to walk.

TEMPORAL LOBE

BRAIN STEM
Damage to the brain stem can cause breathing and swallowing problems. It can also lead to dizziness, nausea, and an irregular heartbeat.

UNDERSTANDING THE DAMAGE

AFTER CANDACE WOKE UP, neurologists performed tests to understand what areas of her brain had been injured. The tests also showed the level of brain damage.

First, the structure of Candace's injured brain was examined with an MRI (magnetic resonance imaging). An MRI produces images by sending short bursts of radio waves into a body part. These radio waves cause the small bits of water in human tissue to give off radio signals. A computer records and analyzes the signals. The computer then makes an image of that part of the body.

On the opposite page, you can compare an MRI of a healthy brain with that of a brain that has suffered a TBI.

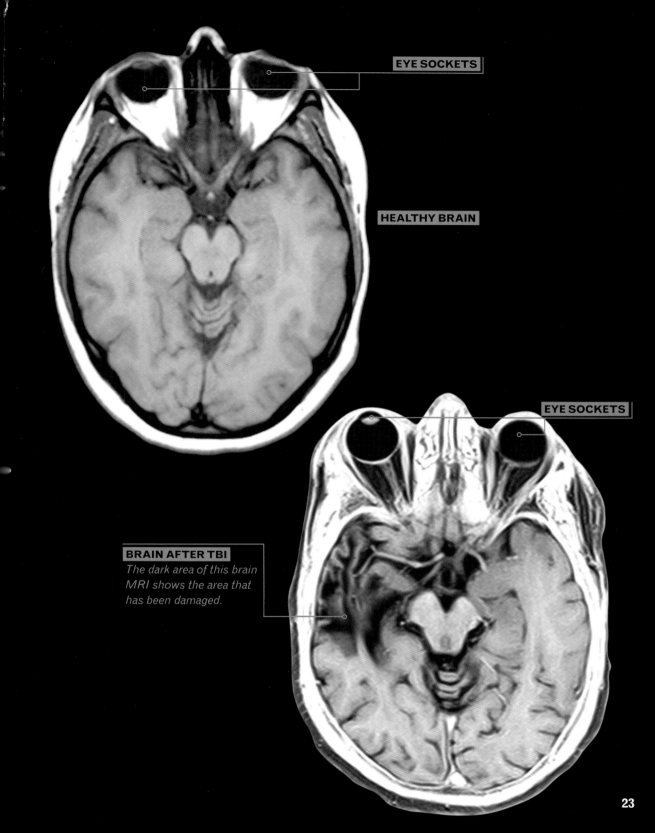

EYE SOCKETS

HEALTHY BRAIN

EYE SOCKETS

BRAIN AFTER TBI
The dark area of this brain MRI shows the area that has been damaged.

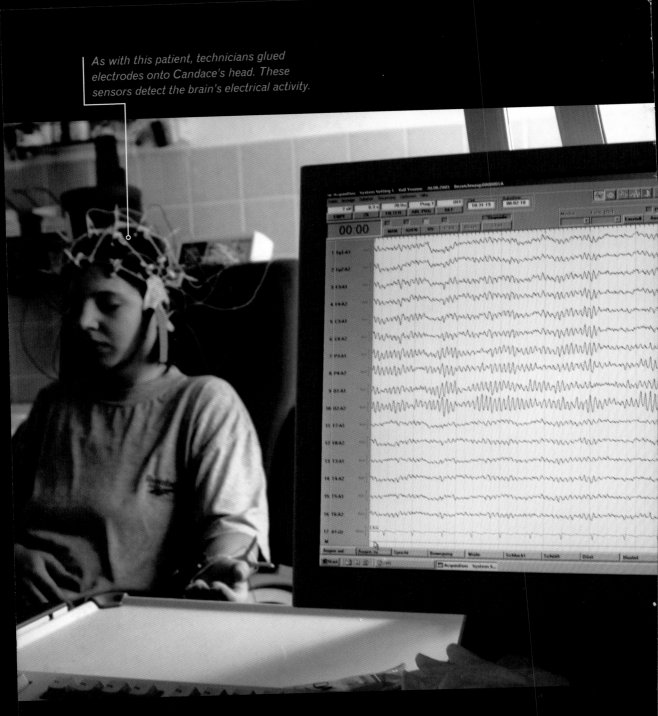

As with this patient, technicians glued electrodes onto Candace's head. These sensors detect the brain's electrical activity.

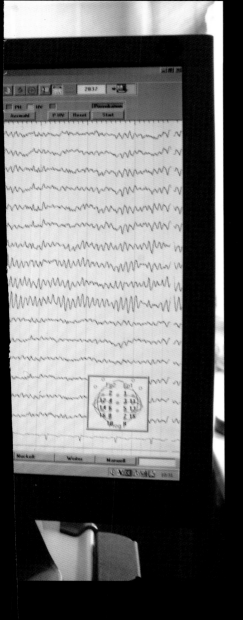

The neurologists also ordered an exam of Candace's brain using a procedure called an EEG (electroencephalogram). During an EEG, sensors called electrodes record the electrical signals the brain gives off.

During this test, Candace had six specific activities to perform: listening to new information, relaxing, reading, memorizing something, recalling something, and making a decision. During each activity, a computer recorded the strength and number of signals per second that Candace's brain produced. The results were displayed as a pattern of brain waves on a computer screen.

A normal awake brain emits electrical signals at a frequency of 8 to 13 cycles per second. Slower cycles per second can mean neuron damage. Spiking, a sudden increase in the number of cycles per second, means the person may experience seizures. Mild seizures may only affect memory, making the person seem forgetful or confused. Strong seizures are likely to affect or damage the whole body.

Finally, Candace's brain function was examined using an fMRI (functional magnetic resonance imaging). In an fMRI, short bursts of radio waves are sent into a specific body part. Like a standard MRI, these bursts stimulate water molecules in the body, especially those in the blood. These molecules give off radio signals. When part of the brain is active, blood flow to that part increases. So the strength of the radio signals from that area increases too. A computer analyzes these signals to create an image.

During this exam, Candace also had specific tasks to perform. For example, she had to think about moving her hand and then move her hand. Compare the results of these two different activities.

THINKING ABOUT MOVING A HAND

The red areas in each hemisphere show the parts of the brain that are active when thinking about moving a body part, the hand.

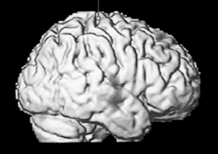 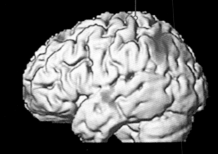

MOVING A HAND

The red areas in the hemispheres show the parts of the brain that are active when actually moving the hand.

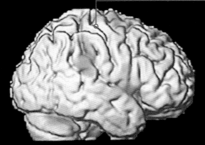 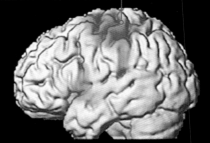

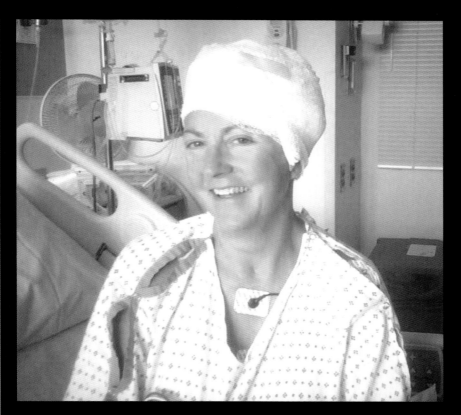

Based on the EEG and MRI tests, Candace's medical team knew she was at risk for seizures. They gave her medication to prevent this from happening. They also saw she had trouble with her sense of balance, coordination, and short-term memory. So Candace began therapy to help her recover. At first she walked with help, and she worked at playing memory games, like Scattergories. Next, she exercised on a stationary bike and played a special electronic game called Brain Age. Later, she was able to go for short walks outdoors. She also worked with a therapist on ways, like making lists, to give her memory a boost.

MISSION RECOVERY

RECOVERING FROM A SEVERE TBI is the toughest duty Lieutenant Colonel Timothy Maxwell has ever done in the U.S. Marine Corps. He's not alone. Of the more than thirty thousand U.S. soldiers wounded in the war in Iraq, medical records show that more than one-fourth have suffered TBIs, mostly from explosions. The results can be life changing. A severe TBI, like the one Tim suffered, means recovery is a lifelong mission.

Tim was injured on October 7, 2004, during his third tour in Iraq. He had just gone off duty and taken off his helmet and armored vest to lie down to sleep. Suddenly, a mortar (explosive device) blew up right outside his tent. The blast shattered his left arm near the elbow. **Two pieces of shrapnel (metal fragments from the mortar) slammed through his left cheek and into his brain.**

Scars are lasting evidence of the wounds Tim Maxwell suffered.

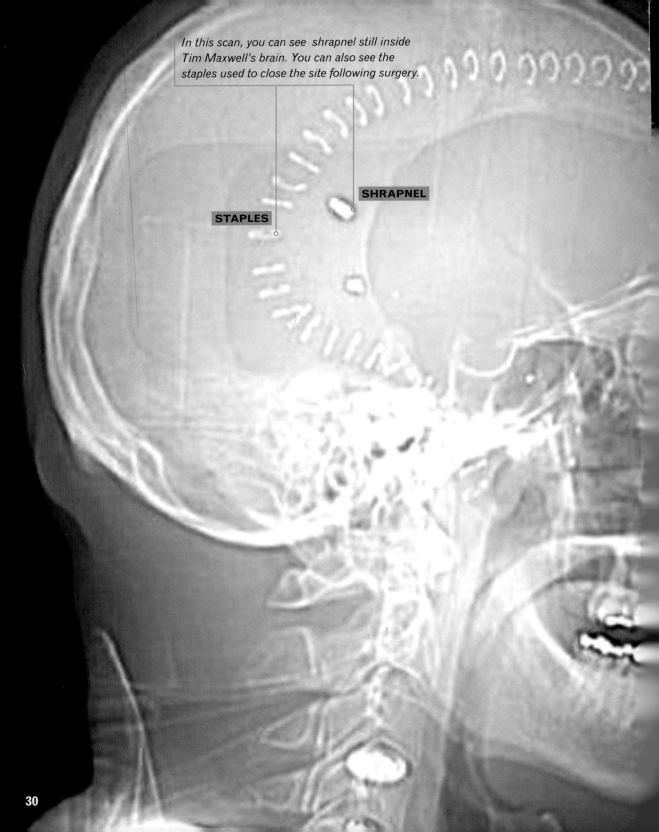

In this scan, you can see shrapnel still inside
Tim Maxwell's brain. You can also see the
staples used to close the site following surgery.

SHRAPNEL

STAPLES

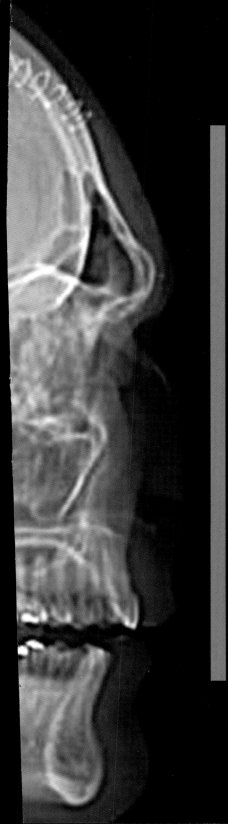

Tim was rushed to the hospital in Baghdad, the capital of Iraq. From there, he was flown to a military hospital in Germany. His arm was repaired. But the surgical team decided not to remove the shrapnel from Tim's brain. The frontal and left temporal areas of Tim's brain had been injured. Surgery to remove the shrapnel could cause even more brain damage. Tim was flown to the United States to recover.

At first, Tim couldn't talk. He had no control over his right side. He also had limited movement on his left side. But Tim's determination to get better wasn't damaged. In an amazingly short time, Tim went from being unable to get out of bed to being in a wheelchair to walking. Soon he was working out, pushing himself to do even more than his trainers asked.

Tim's wife, Shannon, said, "One of the hardest things for Tim was thinking of the right word to call something. Alexis and Eric [their daughter and son] helped by making flash cards to quiz him. Tim also had to learn to read again. Eric was seven and learning to read at the time. So he and his dad practiced reading together."

Tim's progress seemed remarkable. Then, in 2006, in spite of the medications he was on, he suffered a severe seizure. He had to learn to walk all over again. And he had to work on recovering his memory skills again. As determined as before, Tim got off to a good start.

Then he began having more trouble than usual remembering. Soon he had trouble talking and moving. Medical tests showed that one of the pieces of shrapnel in Tim's brain was breaking down. It was leaking toxins (poisons). In 2008 Tim had to undergo surgery to remove that piece of shrapnel. After the surgery, he had to start over yet again, learning to walk and to talk. He also had to struggle to remember things.

Tim's wife, Shannon, listens to the story of the wife of another U.S. marine. Shannon has made helping the families of wounded soldiers her mission.

Every day, Tim tackles his recovery like a military mission. He continues to work hard at it. His family has continued to support him every step of the way. Shannon also formed a support group to help the wives and families of other wounded soldiers. She said, "It's important to understand that our soldiers who come back wounded are still a valuable part of the community. These injuries aren't stops to life. They're just challenges."

HELP FOR NEURONS

SOLDIERS LIKE TIM MAXWELL AND OTHER PEOPLE IN WAR ZONES SUFFER TBIs FROM BOMB AND GRENADE EXPLOSIONS. Researchers are exploring new ways to treat the damage the explosions cause to two nerves in the ear that connect to the brain: the vestibular nerve, which controls balance, and the cochlear nerve, which controls hearing. One treatment approach is to use an infrared laser the size of a speck of dust to stimulate damaged nerves. First, researchers implant an array (cluster) of lots of tiny lasers in the brain to stimulate the damaged nerve. Next, they activate the laser array. The researchers then look to see if the damaged nerves respond with improved balance or hearing. **They hope that the laser array treatment will make damaged nerves function normally again.**

Researchers are also working to find ways to prevent neurons from being damaged after a TBI. Dr. Thomas Glenn is part of a team studying how a chemical called lactate could help. Lactate is a waste chemical that muscles produce when they are working hard.

Under normal conditions, the main energy source for neurons and all the body's other cells is glucose, a kind of sugar. Dr. Glenn's team discovered that when the brain is under stress, it takes in lactate. This becomes another important fuel source to keep the brain cells working.

Dr. Glenn says, "Lactate actually generates energy faster and more efficiently than glucose. So we believe giving patients a fairly high dose of lactate within the first forty-eight hours following a TBI could help neurons survive. And that would prevent brain damage."

Lactate is a waste chemical produced by hardworking muscles. Lactate could provide important energy to the brain's neurons after a person suffers a TBI.

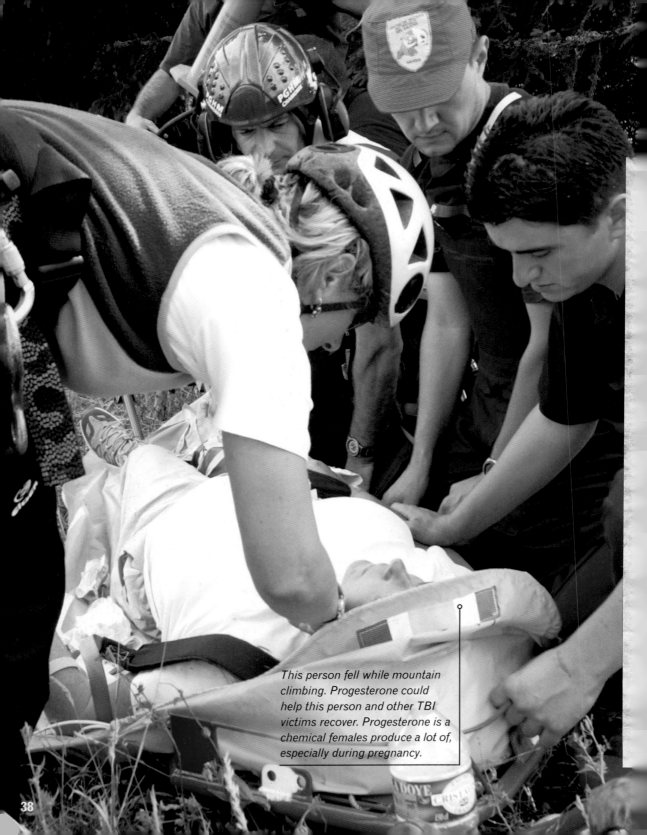

This person fell while mountain climbing. Progesterone could help this person and other TBI victims recover. Progesterone is a chemical females produce a lot of, especially during pregnancy.

Dr. Donald Stein and his team have discovered another chemical that helps prevent neuron damage in the brain—progesterone. In males, this chemical hormone is produced in small amounts. However, it is produced in large amounts in females, especially during pregnancy. While the baby is developing in the womb, progesterone protects developing cells from being attacked by the mother's immune system. Dr. Stein says, "I picked up on the value of progesterone in preventing brain damage when I discovered more women than men survive following severe traumatic brain injuries."

Years of testing the use of progesterone to treat TBIs has shown it reduces brain swelling following a head injury. This helps protect neurons from damage. Progesterone may soon become standard treatment for a TBI.

Medical research, engineering, and technology are enabling doctors to save people who once might have died from traumatic brain injuries. With the help of science, doctors are also helping TBI survivors lead full, active lives.

MELODY GARDOT SUFFERED A SEVERE TBI WHEN SHE WAS STRUCK BY A CAR WHILE RIDING HER BIKE. She struggled with memory loss. Melody said, "I'd either eat four or five meals a day or none at all because I couldn't remember if I'd eaten. I flooded the bathroom repeatedly because I'd brush my teeth and forget to turn off the water. My home was a mess because I had to leave everything out where I could see it in order to find it. For me, out of sight truly was out of mind."

Melody also struggled to put words together in sentences to express her thoughts. Her doctor, Dr. Richard T. Jermyn, suggested she try singing her sentences. She did, and it helped. One day she turned her sentences into a song. Then she wrote more songs. A friend put several of her songs on a MySpace website page on the Internet. A disc jockey at a local radio station in Philadelphia, Pennsylvania, discovered this website. Melody was invited to sing at a benefit concert. To her amazement, that event led to a recording contract. Since then Melody has performed for audiences around the world. She said, "I sometimes forget lyrics while I'm singing. One thing I never forget is how lucky I am."

UPDATES

IN 2008 CANDACE GANTT COMPLETED A HALF-IRON TRIATHLON—70 miles (112 kilometers) of running, biking, and swimming. It was the first major event she'd competed in since her accident. Just by finishing the race, she was a winner.

LIEUTENANT COLONEL TIMOTHY MAXWELL

felt lucky to have a family to help him in his recovery. He worried about wounded soldiers without that kind of support. So he worked to find a way to help them. Due to his efforts, the Marine Corps' Camp Lejeune in North Carolina now has a wounded warrior barracks. It was named Maxwell Hall in Tim's honor. There, injured soldiers live together and support one another as they get well.

KEEP YOUR BRAIN SAFE

These tips will help you avoid suffering a traumatic brain injury:

- Wear a seat belt any time you ride in a motor vehicle.

- Wear a helmet every time you ride a bike, motorcycle, all-terrain vehicle, or snowmobile.

- Wear a helmet whenever you're on a skateboard or a horse.

- Wear a helmet any time you play contact sports, such as football or ice hockey.

- Use the handrail and take one step at a time on stairs.

- Keep home hallways free of tripping hazards, such as throw rugs and toys.

THE BRAIN IS AMAZING!

- Even a badly injured brain doesn't feel pain. The brain lacks pain sensors.

- Tests show your brain is active even while you're asleep. During dreams, the brain is as active as when you're awake.

- The more you learn, the more synapses (connections) develop between neurons, helping you remember what you learned. Some people can remember more than others. A Korean boy named Kim Ung-Yong spoke four languages and could solve complicated mathematical problems by the time he was five years old.

- The brain can process information at an amazingly fast rate. For example, for you to see, light enters your eye and strikes certain cells on the retina at the back of the eye. The cells struck by the light react by emitting electrical signals that travel to the brain. Then the brain analyzes these signals and fills in any missing information, using memories of previous images. This entire process happens in just 50 milliseconds—about one-sixth as long as it takes to blink.

GLOSSARY

axon: the long fiber of a neuron that conducts impulses away from the cell body

brain stem: the part of the brain at the base of the skull that is responsible for passing signals to and from the brain. It controls all automatic body functions, including breathing, heart rate, and digestion.

cerebellum: the part of the brain responsible for keeping the body balanced and coordinated in its movements

cerebrospinal fluid: the fluid around the brain and spinal cord

cerebrum: the part of the brain responsible for thinking, memory, and analyzing sensory signals

coma: a state of consciousness in which a person seems to be asleep and does not respond to anything or anyone

cortex: the surface of the cerebrum

dendrite: the branchlike parts of a neuron that conduct impulses toward the cell body

EEG (electroencephalogram): a process of recording and measuring the electrical activity of the brain

fMRI (functional magnetic resonance imaging): a type of MRI that shows which areas of the brain are active when a person is thinking or performing specific behaviors, such as talking or listening

glial cells: clusters of cells that surround and support neurons

gray matter: another name for the cortex of the cerebrum. The cortex is made up of neuron cell bodies. They look pink in a living brain and gray after death.

intracranial pressure monitor: an instrument for monitoring pressure on the brain due to fluid buildup

meninges: the three layers of tissue that surround and protect the brain and spinal cord

MRI (magnetic resonance imaging): a procedure for producing images by sending short bursts of radio waves into a part of the body. These waves stimulate the water in human tissue to give off tiny radio signals. A computer analyzes these signals and generates an image of the body part.

myelin: the shiny, white fat that surrounds neuron axons

nerves: bundles of fibers made up of neurons that reach most body parts. Some carry signals from body parts to the brain, and others carry signals from the brain to body parts.

neurologist: a medical doctor specializing in the human nervous system

neuron: a nerve cell

seizure: abnormal electrical activity in the brain that causes convulsions, loss of consciousness, or other sensory abnormalities. Seizures range from mild to severe.

skull: the twenty-two bones of the head that surround the brain. The skull supports the face and protects the head and brain from injury.

spinal cord: the thick cord of nerve tissue connecting the brain with nerves coming from and going to every body part

synapse: chemical bridge linking neurons

traumatic brain injury (TBI): damage to the brain caused by a person's head being hit, shaken hard, or punctured. TBIs affect how the brain functions. They may also change how a person acts, moves, and thinks.

white matter: part of the brain below the cortex (surface of the cerebrum). It appears white because it is mainly made of neuron axons, which are surrounded by shiny white myelin (fat).

MORE INFORMATION

Want to learn more about TBIs and the latest medical advancements for treating brain injuries? Check these resources.

BOOKS

Fleischman, John. *Phineas Gage: A Gruesome but True Story about Brain Science*. Boston: Houghton Mifflin, 2002. Discover the true story of a man who survived an iron rod shot through his brain. Learn how this man's experience helped scientists learn more about the human brain.

Landau, Elaine. *Head and Brain Injuries (Diseases and People)*. Berkeley Heights, NJ: Enslow Publishers, 2002. Investigate more about brain injuries, including a historical overview of treatment.

Spilsbury, Richard. *The Brain and Nervous System*. Portsmouth, NH: Heinemann, 2008. Investigate how the human brain and the nervous system work together.

WEBSITES
Brain Connection
http://www.brainconnection.com/ Explore the site to investigate the brain's anatomy, learn what researchers are studying about the brain, play games to exercise your brain, and more.

The Brain Injury Association: Kids Corner
http://www.biausa.org/Pages/for
_kids.html
This site offers facts about brain injury, links, and games to help you think about ways to guard your brain.

Experiments and Activities
http://fc.units.it/ppb/NeuroBiol/
Neuroscienze%20per%20tutti/experi
.html
This site offers games to play, models to build, and lots of experiments to perform while investigating the brain and the nervous system.

The Secret Life of the Brain
http://www.pbs.org/wnet/brain/
episode2/index.htmlhttp://www.pbs
.org/wnet/brain/episode2/index.html
This site is a vast resource focusing on the brain's function from infancy through old age. Additional material includes brain anatomy, the history of brain research, and modern tests for studying the brain.

SELECTED BIBLIOGRAPHY

The sources below are selected from the many resources used during the research for and writing of this book.

BOOKS
Newquist, H. P. *The Great Brain Book: An Inside Look at the Inside of Your Head*. New York: Scholastic Reference, 2004.

Schoenbrodt, Lisa, ed. *Children with Traumatic Brain Injury: A Parent's Guide*. Bethesda, MD: Woodbine House, 2001.

NEWSPAPER
Winerip, Michael. "Holding on to Hope." *New York Times*, February 10, 2008.

http://www.nytimes.com/2008/
02/10/nyregion/nyregionspecial2
/10Rparent.html?_r=1&scp=1&sq
=Holding%20on%20to%20
Hope&st=cse (April 21, 2010).

WEBSITES
Brinley, Maryann. "Battling Traumatic Brain Injury." *University of Medicine and Dentistry of New Jersey Magazine*. 2008.http://www.umdnj.edu/umcweb/
marketing_and_communications/
publications/umdnj_magazine/
spring2008/1.htm (November 10, 2008).

Medical News Today. "Progesterone Promising Treatment for Traumatic Brain Injuries." Emory University. October 6, 2006. http://
www.medicalnewstoday.com/
articles/53275.php (November 10, 2008).

VideoJug. "The Latest Developments in Traumatic Brain Injury Treatment." VideoJug. N.d. http://www.videojug
.com/film/the-latest-developments-
in-traumatic-brain-injury-treatment
(November 10, 2008).

TELEPHONE INTERVIEWS
Cox, Charles, October 23, 2008.

Fellus, Jonathan, December 20, 2008.

Gantt, Candace, September 23, 2008.

Gardot, Melody, October 6, 2008.

Glenn, Thomas, October 30, 2008.

Maxwell, Shannon, July 22, 2009.

Morris, Matthew, October 1, 2008.

Sannino, Bess-Lyn, November 16, 2008.

Smith, Douglas, September 10, 2008.

Spiess, Bruce, October 10, 2008.

Stein, Donald, October 20, 2008.

INDEX

PHOTO CREDITS